Death of a Bodybuilder

A body, the owner of a gym, is found outside the back door to an auto repair shop.

He was generally disliked, but who would kill him? Why?

Was he a blackmailer?

Contents

About the author

CD Moulton has traveled extensively over much of the world both in the music business, where he was a rock guitarist, songwriter and arranger and in an import/export business. He has been everything from a bar owner to auto salvage (junkyard) manager, longshoreman to high steel worker, orchid grower to landscaper, tropical fish farmer to commercial fisherman. He started writing books in 1983 and has published more than 350 books as of January 1, 2023. His most popular books to date are about research with orchids, though much of his science fiction and fantasy work has proven popular. He wrote the CD Grimes, PI series, and the Det. Nick Storie series, Clint Faraday series, and many other works.

He now resides in Gualaca, Chiriqui, Panamá, where he writes books, plays music with friends, does research with orchids and medicinal plants. He has lately become involved in fighting for the rights of the indigenous people, who are among his closest friends, and in fighting the extreme corruption in the courts and police in Panamá.

He offers the free e-book, *Fading Paradise*, that explains what he has been through because of the corruption.

CD is the discoverer of the Chadam Protocol for curing cancer.

Facebook page Ambrosia peruviana for cancer.

Geofrey (GJ) James Franklin groaned and looked at the clock.

5:28 AM

He sighed and waited two minutes for the alarm to go off, then got up, went into the kitchen (such as it was) to turn on the coffee machine, then went to the bathroom for the morning routine.

There wasn't much light coming in the little window in the kitchen/ dinette. It was 5:51, so it was going to be a pretty dreary morning. Like yesterday. Cloudy and a little drizzly, like it couldn't decide whether to rain or clear up.

Not six o'clock yet and depressing. It was, at least, cool enough now. It would get fairly hot and humid by nine and put people in murderous moods.

GJ was sheriff in a little town with a name nobody could pronounce except the Indians. Mathonamesales, New Mexico. He had one night deputy and one day deputy. And a sort of secretary/desk sgt, Maria Lonefox.

Well, he was the typical Mexican Border area cop, to look at. Tall, lanky, brown hair and eyes, a ready smile and as ready scowl, good friend or dangerous enemy.

He didn't have many enemies, thank whatever gods he didn't believe in. He was an easy-going sort. He'd learned to let things settle on their own as much as possible. He'd much rather reason than arrest. Most of the types of problems he faced were personal disputes that involved yelling and accusations and threats (that were heat-of-the-moment reactions), rarely going into more. He would talk to the people and make them see reason and that this crap didn't solve problems.

If it was too close to becoming violent, everyone in the area knew it wouldn't continue. When he stepped in "officially" he was going to be the hard-ass type.

He had drawn his sidearm exactly twice in his four and a half year stint here. Once at a holdup, where he established how far he would go when it came to death threats to innocent people. The two holdup men has a woman teller held in front of them, threatening to kill her if they weren't allowed to pass. The woman had tried to twist out of the hold and the thug had grabbed her hair and yanked her off her feet – which meant she wasn't in the line of fire anymore. GJ drew and fired faster than you could see. He was a dead accurate shot. The hood dropped with a hole between his eyes not ten mm from dead center. The other one snapped a shot at GJ that missed him no more than six inches.

He didn't get a chance at a second shot.

The next day's headlines in the local newspaper – aptly named "The Daily Gossip" – read, *You Don't Mess with Wyatt Earp! Our sheriff doesn't take mercy on violent criminals.*

The story made it seem like an old-time shoot-out.

The other time was when some idiot pedophile from Taos had come to town and was caught with a scared little girl behind the supermarket. Mrs. Tigerpaw heard the little girl crying and had called. GJ had run from his office the three blocks to the market, around back, had seen the man about to rape the little (7 years old) girl.

That one dropped, GJ grabbed the little girl and got her out of there before it could register what had happened, then went back. The rapist wasn't quite dead, according to the stories. There was a second shot. Nobody ever asked about it. Child molestation was the one act everyone in the area had zero tolerance for.

The headlines read: *Child Molesters, Warning! Go Anywhere Else In the World Before You Come Here!*

The state cops investigated, then the FBI.

Ranting about civil rights.

GJ (and the whole town) said they were more concerned with victim's rights.

No one found any evidence against GJ. The FBI coroner said either shot was fatal. The first one would allow the one who was shot to live perhaps six or eight minutes, so whether the second was right then or a couple of minutes later meant nothing.

As Wanda Redbird said, "I hope he was alive and knew that second one was coming and why!"

No one else ever went far enough to even chance GJ would draw that sidearm. They had seen him perform at the yearly rodeo, where he took the first place for quickness and accuracy. Everyone said there was no place for a second place because no one else ever came close in either time or accuracy, so they should have a first and third and leave the second out.

He was known to step into a brawl and show the brawlers how it was done. He said there was no excuse for getting physical unless it was someone from "outside" who started it, then you kick their ass until their nose bleeds.

There were those down by Eastend Street who were into violence in some ways, more or less teenage and early twenty gang mentality types. They knew exactly how far they could go. They didn't cross that line. If they wanted to go out back and battle it out, fine. Keep it among yourselves. Go too far and GJ would handle it in his own way.

What many people couldn't understand was why those punks and motorcycle bums who he beat hell out of became friends.

"It isn't personal, just Alpha male kind of crap," was GJ's answer. "Contest to see who's alpha. Live with it or try again. If you get your ass kicked enough you eventually learn."

Drugs?

"If it's not addicting and used against you, so what? If it's something like crack, don't even let me get a hint. You *will* find I'm not moveable on that kind of stuff. Dealers. If you even try it, you're stupid beyond belief. If you get hooked on anything, it's not that far to Taos. Dealers run the risk of going to Taos, too. In a box."

Things ran smoothly. The town had about four thousand people (though the "official" stats didn't include the two thousand four or five hundred Indians) and enjoyed a peaceful and cooperative culture.

When GJ first was elected, the Indians were treated very differently than now. He made it plain there were no whites or blacks or Asians or Indians, Jews, blacks, Muslims or gentiles in

Mathonamesales. Just people. Live with it or leave.

The result was a place that had close to zero features that would attract a population, but was a place people wanted to stay in.

The desert was different. It had a beauty to a different standard. GJ found it beautiful.

Well, not on a day like today. It almost never rained here, but had a few weeks when it seemed to be threatening to. When it did, sometimes the rain never quite reached the ground. What did was absorbed so fast it never seemed to even dampen anything. About once in four years there was a rainstorm that washed out gorges and caused a lot of damage. It was so flat it had nowhere to drain to, so cut its own path. It was amazing to GJ how many plants sprung up almost overnight after such a storm. Frogs and bugs appeared from nowhere. A few days later, the plants had seeded and were dead, there were no more frogs or bugs, it was hot and dry.

Or cold. It got cold at night parts of the year.

Not this time of year.

GJ finished the morning routine and took his big thermos of fresh strong black coffee to the truck, waved to the Whitehorse kids on their way to the school bus stop, got in the old GMC, and headed for town.

At the office, Tom Marvin was sleeping in the cell. Nobody else there.

"Drunk or stoned?" GJ asked Billy Greyeagle, the night deputy.

"Neither. He asked if he could sleep here and I said it was okay. He does a couple times a month, anyway."

"Don't let him think he can move in. We need the cell sometimes."

"No. I said only last night."

GJ nodded. There were no reports on the desk.

"Dull. Like we want it to be," Billy said. "You always said we should work for the day we don't have a job because we had eliminated the reason for it."

Tom Lester, day deputy, came in to greet them. They chatted for a few minutes, then Billy went home to his wife and daughter. Tom didn't have a wife. He had a boyfriend.

GJ didn't consider that any of his business, either.

There was a call that a couple of teenage boys were getting loud and about to start fighting at the school, so Tom went to tell them to grow up. It would be about some girl or something as typical.

GJ caught up on the files, which was only to okay what Maria had already done.

Maria came in at eight. She brought a big basket

with things to weave a blanket. She made the thread at home and had a little type of loom in the storeroom. Her work was artistic and really beautiful. She had been offered more than two thousand dollars for one by a tourist from California who came through and saw her showing it to Matty Burningbush. He said he owned a store that sold Persian rugs that weren't half the quality for twice the price.

She said it was for a gift. Lenia Burningbush was getting married to Henry Flintwater. It wasn't for sale.

GJ loved these unassuming, warm people.

A bit of reading for awhile. A Nick Storie mystery. GJ liked the way Nick operated and liked the way the police department in Naples worked, though he knew this was fiction and a million miles from any police department that was really like that.

At noon he and Maria closed the office with a sign that said they were at Lottie's Lunch, if there was a reason.

When they were seated and had ordered, Franko Benetti, a motorcycle rider from Eastend Street came in. He had some bandages and tapes.

"What? Stood up when they said shut up?" GJ asked.

Franko laughed. "Basically, that ain't far from

what happened. I let my Gila Monster mouth overload my gecko ass. Taos. Not here."

"Gonna be reprisals?"

"No. They ain't comin' here with you here. It was about some stuff I bought that wasn't, shall we say, up to snuff."

"Yeah. Lennie was complaining about the bad pot they got last week," Maria said. "You let those little skinx smack you around that bad?"

"No. I don't want to say what it was 'cause you won't believe me."

"What?" GJ asked.

"I ran my mouth to three of them. Two are worse-off than me."

"I believe you," Maria said. "You're about that stupid."

He laughed and gave her the bird. She grinned.

"Buen provecho!" Franko said, and left.

"Bet there isn't anyplace else in this country where a motorcycle hood can come into a restaurant and tell the sheriff he got his ass kicked over a drug deal and get sympathy," Maria said.

"Pot isn't drugs. Not to my way of thinking, and he didn't get any sympathy."

She laughed.

Several of the Indian women came to look over the place, then to come to tell GJ that there was going to be trouble. Some preacher wanted to open a church in their neighborhood. He was from Macon, Georgia, and didn't know shit about them. They didn't want him raving on to the children.

"He has a right to open his church anywhere he wants," GJ answered. "It's really very easy. You have a right to see your children are removed from a negative influence. Nobody go to his church and let him know he is not to speak to children under ten years old if they are not with a parent. By that age they know bullshit when they hear it.

"If he tries to talk to them anyway, show him the old paper about what happens to pedophiles. When he's shocked and dismayed that you think he's a pedophile, tell him that's what it's beginning to look like."

"What if he won't go?"

"I have a little trick or two," GJ assured her.

"I don't think he's a child molester, but he talks like he's gay," one of them said. "It might seem that way because all preachers sound like they're gay to me."

GJ shrugged. "That's his business. He keeps it away from children."

"My boy is just fourteen. What if he tries any-thing with my boy?" one asked.

"You raised the boy to say, 'No,' if he's not

interested, didn't you?"

She grinned. "Yeah. I think there's already been a time he didn't say no."

They all laughed. GJ said to let him know if things went past a certain point and he'd find a way to settle it.

They went back to the office. GJ finished the mystery and his coffee. He said he would walk around a bit to see what was going on in town. He was almost to the door when Danolo Garcia ran in to say that George Wright was dead! He was murdered!

"George Wrangle? Isn't he the guy with the gym?" Maria asked.

"Yeah. Big handsome guy who thought any woman in six counties was dreaming of him at night," Danolo replied. "Donna Burke said he's lousy in bed. Thinks you should be so glad he was there you would think it's the best ever."

"I'll go. Tom is busy. Where? The gym?"

"No. Back of Phil's Auto Shop. Eastend and Cactus."

"Okay. Office is yours, Maria."

"Whoopie."

GJ went to the GMC and to the auto shop. There were a few people walking around. The body was just outside the back door. He had been, from what GJ could see, hit over the head with something, then a wire wrapped around his neck and twisted tight. Bloody left side of head and the wire was right there. Not many would be able to do it with him conscious.

He called the clinic and asked that Dr. Tenn come over. He was the nearest thing they had to a coroner. GJ was the police department and CSI.

He did study forensics, so wasn't totally at a loss.

"How many of you came back here before I got here?" he asked the people milling around. He made a careful video of all of them. It was true quite often that a killer would return to the scene of the crime, if just to be sure some clue wasn't left to point to him.

"Just Lenny," Jimmy Tate, the only other mechanic at the shop,

GJ nodded. He took his camera from the GMC and took pictures of every inch back there and of the body from every angle he could. Doc came and checked over the body. He said, "He's dead. Blow to head possibly caused a severe concussion, but he died from the wire around his neck. No marks indicating defense. Area not seriously disturbed.

"Theory, until something better comes along: He was with someone or waiting for someone, was struck forcefully on the left temple of his head, dropped, and the wire was placed and twisted.

"I would estimate TOD at ... eight to ten and a half hours ago. It is two twenty three PM. Time to be determined after adjustment at the lab.

"Identity to be confirmed at the lab.

"That's about what I can do here. A couple of you help Enrique bag and transport.

"Anything else, GJ? I'm supposed to be doing a hernia seal."

"No. Thanks, Doc. I'll give you the time to finish whatever needs finishing."

They bagged the body and put it in the delivery van used as an ambulance and drove off. GJ took pictures of where the body had been laying. He searched and found a couple of quarters and a cigar band – that could have been there for days.

You never know.

He bagged the "evidence" and headed for the station. Tom was there, filling out a report.

"That Basquins kid is headed for trouble. Him again. Finding out that all the smaller kids aren't scared of him. Got a black eye and kneed in the balls just before I got there. Oscar Yellowbird may be small and skinny, but he would probably put Basquins in the hospital if I hadn't gotten there when I did."

"Basquin? Sam Basquins' kid? Wants to be called Wolf, or is, or something?!

"His name is Wolf. Uh-huh."

"Shit! So now we'll get Sam in here whining that six or seven of the biggest kids in the school ganged up on his p-o-o-o-o-o-or innocent little angel. Shit!"

"Only I got the pictures from a couple of phones that show that ain't how it went down, Charlie!

The type needs to learn that most of those kids carry Blackberries or whatever and will take a video when some crud starts something."

GJ and Tom did a palm slap. Basquin was known to be the model for his punky bully son.

"I'll wait for Papa dear to whine, with sonny-boy sitting there looking innocent, then show the whole thing on the comp," Tom suggested. "We can maybe show them how those things go, now."

"Then he'll wait somewhere to waylay the smaller kids where other won't see it," GJ warned.

"Kids who will expect it because someone they won't name told them to carry a defense," Tom countered. "If every little runt he tries to bully kicks his ass he may learn ... nah!"

"Well, we have a murder to solve. Maybe it won't be quite so dull for awhile."

The phone rang. Maria said it was Doc, at the clinic. Seems some kid got a serious kneeing. Two other kids held him while a third one kneed him in the groin. There might be permanent damage, so Doc called."

"Tom and I will go over there," GJ said. "Might be interesting!"

GJ and Tom went to the clinic to find Sam Basquins and son there, son on a Gurney. Doc repeated about what Maria reported. Tom winked at GJ and went on down the hall a short distance. GJ went into the examination room

"Doc, I'll take a report. This is serious. You know how I am about violence among those kids. If any of them are into starting something that will end in violence I want to know about it, and I'll put an end to it!

"Can I use your computer?"

"My computer? Er, yes, but why?"

"Take the report with the spycam and all, print it out, they sign.

"I would have brought the office comp, but there was a murder. Maria is using it."

Doc could see Tom grinning from just outside the door. He said they could use the one on the desk. It was free, for the moment. He had to go to the lab, so it was up to the police. GJ gave him the quarters and cigar band.

GJ turned to the Basquins, and declared, "This is an official police procedure to take a complaint about a physical conflict that ended with injuries. Do you swear to tell the truth, the whole truth, and nothing but the truth?"

Both of them said, "Yes."

"Very well. You are speaking under oath. Tell me, in your own words, as shortly as you can, what happened."

"My son was coming out of the school and got

jumped by three or four of them and they held him and beat him up and even crushed one of his balls!" Sam yelled.

"Not you. I want firsthand information, not what you think happened.

"Wolf, is it? Tell me what happened."

"What Dad said. Four or maybe five of them. They put a thing over my head and held me and beat me up! I know the one who kneed me! I know his voice and he even said it was him! Oscar Yellowbird! That's who! There were two of them holding me and I couldn't do anything or even see them!"

"You swear that is truth, under penalty of perjury?"

"Uh, yeah, what I said."

"An officer came. Did you report that to him?"

"Uh, he came just after and they ran away. I was hurting. I don't remember what I said."

"I see.

"Tom! Are you close?"

Tom came into the room. Papa said he would be able to say what was true! Wolf looked like he would pass out.

"Yo, GJ. What?"

"You said you had evidence about a violence case when we left the office. I haven't had time to see any of it. We came right over.

"Can you show me the evidence and report?"

"Yeah. It's recorded. Can I put it on the comp? It's on a memory stick."

"Yeah. He came just after Yellowbird kneed me!"

"Just as," Tom corrected. "Two of the students there had Blackberries and made a video of what happened. I suppose Wolf told you he picked on the wrong smaller kid, this time."

"It's a lie!" Sam yelled.

"YEEEE! Dad!"

"A video? A lie?" GJ asked.

"Two. From different angles," Tom replied.

Wolf started crying. Sam looked more than a little scared.

"Uh, you mean you didn't tell me the truth? Why would you lie to me, Son? You mean what I said wasn't true *because you told me a lie*? Is that it?"

Wolf didn't answer.

"You know something, GJ? I think maybe he told Papa the truth and Papa made up what he was supposed to say to us. I think maybe Papa is suborning perjury here."

"I just wanted to make them pay the doctor bills! I wouldn't bring any charges! I can't afford the doctor bill!" Sam whined.

"Perjury suborning is automatic two years, isn't it?" Tom asked.

Sam squealed.

"Tell you what. You shut the fuck up and stop teaching your kid to be a bully, seeing he has a lesson he won't forget the rest of his life that should teach him not everyone smaller than him can be intimidated, and we'll pretend this didn't happen.

"I'm going to keep the evidence. If we get anymore shit from you, about anything, I just might go over a few cold cases. Got it?" GJ asked with a hard look.

"Mumble, mumble."

Tom and GJ went back to the office.

"Well, that still leaves us with the murder," GJ said. "I suppose we'd better first check with people he knew or who worked out at the gym or whatever. We don't have a direction."

"Maybe we'd better get to the gym and see what's happening there. He wasn't there to open this morning, so someone should have noticed something," Tom suggested.

"Yeah. I don't have experience with homicide from an investigation angle, but I took all the courses at the academy. We have to locate anything that gives us a hint of anything.

"Did that make sense to you? It didn't to me."

"In a sort of weird way."

GJ went to the auto repair shop. Jimmy Tate was there, but Phil Collins (not that one. The owner) was in Taos to pick up some parts. There wasn't any business, except for a rebuild on Karen Songbird's Jeep, and Phil would be bringing the parts for that. Just a couple of oil changes and like that.

Jimmy said there were a lot of parts being stolen lately. Could GJ look into that?

He said he would. He thought of something. "Did Wrangle have a car?"

"Yeah. A seventy nine Mustang. He got oil changes and special parts from here. Some special stuff for his car was stolen. He had the only one around here, so it couldn't have been most people. Who stole them."

The gym was open and running. Two fat women were on the bicycles, chatting and drinking sodas. Tom rolled his eyes and grinned. Nan Garratt, the one in charge of programs for women, very quietly said, "Burn off three hundred calories while drinking eight hundred in those sodas, and they'll probably drink a couple more before the end of the exercise. Then it's our fault they actually *gained* weight on our weight loss program!

"Is it true George is dead?"

"Yeah," GJ answered. "He was murdered out

back of the auto repair on Eastend."

"*Murdered*?! I thought is was some kind of accident!"

"Hit over the head and a wire wrapped around his neck," Tom said. "Do you know anyone who would want him dead?"

"A few, but they would just want him dead. They wouldn't kill him. The Indians don't like him. He's a bigot."

"Who, not Indian, and any Indian who was particularly pissed at him for anything?"

"Willie and Alma Stebbens. He called them a couple of porkers without the willpower to better themselves. Lyle Benson, because he always called him a screaming fag. Sarah Gladstone was his latest dumped conquest. Andy Little, because he was messing with his daughter, Brenda.

"Oh! John Wang, because he was always calling him a Chink. He didn't reserve his bigotry.

"Morris Greenberg and Cal Glass. Ditto reasons.

"Reverend Arvin Aaron AlfredCartwright, but he would just damn him to eternal hell and fire, Brethens and cisterns, Amen!

"I think John would kick his ass pretty soon. He's really good at taekwando.

"They would all like to kick his ass. I don't think they thought he was worth killing, except the Right Reverend, and he'd get God's help by having someone else take retribution."

GJ nodded. "You? You don't like Cartwright, I take it."

"No. He was just a narcissist and pathetic. We got along. Had to. Business. Nothing else.

"Cartwright's so pious and holier-than-thou you want to shove his Bible down his throat. Him, I might murder, but it would be slow and painful."

Kalinda Railer, a very pretty black woman, about 22 years old, came in, waved at Nan, and called that she heard the asshole bastard son of a bitchin' dickhead had bought the farm. Nan nodded.

"What happened? He pull his mightier than thou act on the wrong person?"

"Could be," Nan replied.

"Wish I could'a been there. Stick him a time or two, myself!"

"You think he was stuck?" Tom asked.

"Didn't hear no shot. Seems next most likely. He would be hard to beat to death. That would be my choice, if I could."

"He hit on you?" Tom asked.

"He hit on everybody. Sayin' I was just a hot sexy nigger bitch who probably had a lot of experience ain't the best pickup line I can think of, off-hand."

"I don't think I'll bother remembering that one

to try Saturday night," Tom said.

"You'd have a damned lonely Saturday night if you did," Nan said.

They joked a bit. GJ left Tom talking to the women and went to the office. He went through anything that might have given him a direction, but there wasn't much.

Wrangle had an apartment in the building next door. He had a copy of the key Doc found in his pocket, so he slipped out he back door and went there.

The place was a little messy, but not actually dirty. There was a desk with the business papers and so forth in a file cabinet beside it. The files seemed to just be the things a business would keep. The living expenses and so forth were in a drawer marked "Personal."

GJ found a bankbook in that. He would go through it later. He put it in an evidence bag and slipped it into his pocket.

The bedroom was all mirrors. There was a big round bed that took up most of it. There were mirrors on the ceiling.

GJ looked in the closets, two of them. One was a lot of clothes that consisted mainly of muscle shirts and tight jeans. The second had a computer with lines running from a separator in six directions. To small videocameras hidden in light fixtures and mirror decorations.

GJ thought for a moment, then found a box of memory sticks. He put one in the USB port to the computer and turned it on. It was Wrangle in the bed with four different women on that stick. GJ thought he knew who one of those women was. The wife of a local politician. Town council and lawyer for the town.

He thought a minute more and took the bankbook from his rear pocket. He looked at the transactions.

It seemed Wrangle had a source of income that wouldn't be on the tax forms.

GJ took the memory sticks, took videos covering every inch of the apartment, and sealed the entrance with a police seal when he left.

Tom saw the sack he had when he went back to the gym and raised an eyebrow.

"I think, just maybe, I have a motive that won't quit!"

GJ put the last of the memory sticks back into the sack. He had thirty seven probables as to being blackmail victims, any one or combination of whom might be his killer. Wrangle was shown to be the narcissistic jerk Nan and Kalinda had described, but the mirrors told him that, at a glance. He had a list of names that he and Tom had connected with the videos. It was a code in the back of the daily record for the gym, disguised as clients of the gym. A few of them were definitely *not* clients of the gym.

"Tom, let's start a sort of investigation. We'll interview the people who were known to know him and make it seem a matter of chance we interview the women in the videos. I'll copy anything on the memories that may be pertinent, then have an accident with these. Maybe leave the evidence box on the stove while I check outside. How was I to know the damned thing was on?"

Tom nodded. He knew how GJ's mind worked. Why cause a lot of people grief when there was no purpose except maliciousness behind it?

They made a list of major possibilities and a

second that would be handled more casually. Make the meetings look chance.

Maria came in to say a Mrs. Jenkins wanted to speak with him. In private. She seemed to be very upset about something. Had to do with the murder.

Tom saluted and took his list out. GJ said to send Mrs. Jenkins in.

He recognized her the moment she walked into the room. She was on the memory sticks. She didn't seem to be cooperating very well on them.

"We won't need a recording secretary Maria. This is a personal matter.

"Mrs. Jenkins, please have a seat."

Maria went out and closed the door. Mrs. Jenkins fidgeted and said she didn't know how to say what she had to say. It really was personal. It had to do with the murder, and it was personal. Very personal.

"Mrs. Jenkins, we know he was blackmailing people. I have no excuses for blackmail that I'll accept, except personal protection or protection of family in cases where the law can't protect."

"Well, sheriff, that's what it's about. Will the things he has have to come out?

"It would hurt a lot of people who were weak for a moment. People who ... were foolish and stupid and got into a situation they couldn't control."

"Off the record, if I find anything like that in this or any other case, it will evaporate before we can examine it, unless it identifies a criminal, then my testimony would be coercion or force, making it extraordinary circumstances."

She stared at him a moment, then smiled. "You are a good person. What happened was really that. If you find it ... it could only cause harm and pain to people who are not involved. Thank you."

He escorted her to the door, went back to cross her off the second list, and told Maria he and Tom would be investigating. Call him if needed.

When he walked by the 24 Hour Diner he saw Tom talking to Betty Gringham at a table. Tom would probably finish list 2 before list 1. He would drink a lot of coffee and chat with people. He was popular. It would seem chance.

GJ went to talk with Arrow Benttree. He was a sort of chief in the area, and knew what was going on. GJ knew subterfuge would get him nowhere, probably even resistance.

"Hi, Arrow. Looks like a nicer day today."

"It'll clear. More of the water in four days. It's El Niño, according to TV."

"Know anything about Wrangle's murder?"

"Not any of us. He was a sad person without a soul, so he was dead already. Someone brought it to his attention."

"Definite?"

"Yes. I would know, if only because someone would not look me in the eyes. We all know I would not say who it was. No one liked him. We pitied him. He was incomplete. He was all inside himself and felt nothing. Empty inside. Not enough women in the world to fill up the hole where his spirit had left.

"GJ, it is a very sick and sad world anymore. It will not much longer sustain, as it is. I fear greatly when the final change comes. There is no good sign. It will be disaster for all, equally. They are too blind to see that."

"I'm afraid you're right. When it comes, I think this is a better place to be than close to or in any city."

"The cities will be the traps. The results will be to all. Here."

"Here?"

"There are isolated places, some quite large. They are the tropical jungles, mostly here in the Americas, but some in other places. Perhaps some people in those places will not even know what has happened for a time. They will be the new start."

GJ nodded seriously. "Maybe something will evolve that is worth the existence."

"It is a divided path with many forks. It will not

be an easy thing to always take the right one.”

“Perhaps there will be some strong spirits who will direct them.”

“But those spirits will be from now. They will not have the knowledge to direct another time and another group of minds.”

“I think yours will.”

“And yours. We can hope we meet again, then. Together we might make a small difference, do you think?”

“It is our nature to try.”

“Yes. We each will try, even against impossible odds. It is us. It is what we are.”

They embraced. GJ went on toward the center of town.

He was passing the park when, thrill of thrills! The Right Reverend Arvin Aaron Alfred Cartwright came to ask to speak with him about the soul of the poor misguided lost soul who was brutally murdered long before his time, long before he had the time to discover the path to glory and to seek forgiveness for his sordid, Satan-inspired life.

Shit!

“He was knocked over the head an garotted. It wasn’t a particularly brutal murder. Nowhere near heinous. Why not say you wanted to talk about the murdered man?”

"I fear I tend to speak much to formally in situations where there is so much depravity and sin running rampant in the lives...."

"Can it! Just say you are too wordy and know it. Don't try to turn a conversation into a sermon. I don't have the time or patience."

"You are correct. I fear that it is too true that I...."

"You fear too much. Get to the point."

"Er. well, yes. You see, there are people in my congregation who discuss major facets of their lives, particularly when they backslide, with me, and I wish to mediate a solution if my poor abilities will allow to spare further pain and suffering...."

"He was blackmailing some of your flock. Just say that."

"Er, well, it is true that I have received such reports, and that I have agonized greatly, as I know how deeply and widely such sordid...."

"For Christ's sake! Just say it! What?"

"You should chose your words with care. You approach blasphemy a bit closely with that. Your immortal soul....!

"Goodbye. When you decide to say what it is you want to say, look me up. Until then, take your sermons back to your church."

"I have to know if he left some kind of lies about

me that you have found!"

"How do you lie with a video? I haven't looked at many of them yet."

"But he didn't have ... videos? I don't ... Oh, dear God!"

"Just tell me, flat out, what you're so afraid I'll find. If it has nothing to do with the murder or another crime, it will disappear. I promise you and everyone else that will happen."

"It is about my ... backslide ... affair with ... a woman from the church. I don't think any video ... but she would have to ... no. He would have been told by the woman. That's what he said. He had her voice recorded when she told him. He said it would cost me a thousand dollars to have the recording erased."

"After which he would have a few copies he would sell to you when he wanted more. That's how they work."

"I told him I would seek pardon from God, directly, and that God would protect me and forgive my very human backslide.

"Still, for that to come out now would be terribly embarrassing and detrimental to ... you see."

"If it has nothing to do with the murder, it won't ever be found."

"Thank you. I don't deserve it. I agonize greatly for my evil. I believe I have been forgiven."

"Then put it in the past, learn from it, and avoid any other backslides."

"That, I promise both you and the Good Lord. I feel you are a good and compassionate man. God will bless you."

"Take care." GJ walked off. Cartwright was off the list, but not a long way off. That he was capable of having an affair was a surprise. GJ didn't know him as well as he'd thought he did.

Angie Downy came to greet him. She asked if she was any part of the reverend's chat.

"Not directly."

"Indirectly?"

"I couldn't say. It's not easy to pick out anything in what he ... says."

She laughed. "I had a little fling with him. Fuckhead Schtump was trying to blackmail him about it. I told him I would say I told the slimepit that to see what he would do and that it wasn't true. After all, he was a good bedmate, while Scoreboard was lousy in bed.

"I don't pretend to be anything more than I am. I'm not a whore, but I'm not a chaste maiden, either."

GJ couldn't resist. "Cartwright was good in bed?"

She laughed. "I was surprised, too! Damned good!"

Cartwright was definitely worth a little more investigation.

They chatted a bit more. Angie was still on the list. Her only alibi was that she was at the diner, and the only one she talked to was a local drunk, who wouldn't remember he was even there. He was really that drunk.

If anyone tried to blackmail her, she might very well smack them over the head with a pipe or rock and garrote them.

Tom came out of the Food Fancier (a real third class dump) to say Bessie Rauls and Frieda Stoner were off the list. They'd been at a discotheque with Sam Raintree and Don Littlebird. Betty was off, and Harry Ford. they were at the same disco. Raul Quintero was on. He said he got drunk and didn't know which places he was in. He thinks he was alone most of the night.

"Well, Angie Downy and Cartwright are on. All the Indians are off."

"*Cartwright* is on?! Cripes! *Cartwright*?! I can see Angie."

"Something not quite right about him – besides being a pious pain in the ass. Wrangle was trying to blackmail him."

"He did something to be blackmailed for? Hard to believe. Dipping into ... but they're his funds, anyhow."

"A little fling with Angie."

"*Cartwright* had a fling!? Now I've heard everything!"

"She said he was really good in bed."

"Brother! I don't know him at all!"

"Sort of my reaction. It's why he's on the list."

They chatted a little more.

At the end of the day their list consisted of Cartwright, Quintero, Angie, , Pepe Gonzales, Tara Glorine, and Charles Enders.

Next day the list was those plus Eugene Hampton and Mary Sellers.

Tom and GJ went through the memories and the lists. Four of the memory sticks had accidents, immediately. The others had an item or two copied off them, then they had accidents.

Now to shorten the list and to find if there was a missed probability. Everyone in the county was a possibility.

"Maria, I'm going to have to spend some time with Cartwright. I want to leave him until some things are checked out. I'm not sure it would be a good idea to question them here."

"Centertown Restaurant has a private dining room that's pretty well soundproof from outside, and is in the center of town, if the name didn't give that secret away. Lili Greenfrog owns it and says she owes you her life from when you caught that Carlton guy who was stalking her."

"Could be. Call her, will you?"

Maria went to the phone and came back to say he was welcome to use the room anytime it wasn't booked, and it wasn't booked until Friday night.

"Today's Friday," Tom pointed out.

"But it's not Friday night."

"Point taken. We should be through before she needs to start setting up," GJ said. "Charlie Enders is just half a block away, so he's first. I'll go to the restaurant and set it up. Tom can bring Enders in. You can take over the office."

"Whoopie."

GJ went out and was just at the restaurant when Lester Higgins drove by in his GTO. It was a showroom classic. GJ could know he wasn't in town for the murder because that car would have been noted by fifty people.

Wait a minute! I'm overlooking something that could be important! Wrangle had that Mustang. There could be any number of things in that car. Where is it?

He went on inside. Tom called and said he would have Enders there in half an hour.

"Tom? We haven't checked out Wrangles car."

"Yeah. I did. It's in that garage across from his apartment. Nothing at all. A map of the county in the glovecase and a set of keys for the gym and his apartment, hidden in a little box under the right fender behind the headlight gizmo.

"That car was *clean*! I think it had to be about the most important thing in his life."

"You take the pictures?"

"Yeah. Memory stick's in the file. Car, Wrangle."

GJ read over a few notes. He saw it was probably a waste of time questioning Enders. He called Tom and asked him to ask Enders if he went anywhere at two, after the bar he claimed he was in closed. Tom put Enders on.

"Mr. Enders, where did you go after the bar

closed. It was just at that time the murder was taking place. If you went anywhere where you were seen, we have no need to question you further."

"Well, I think I went somewhere. I remember having coffee ... That's right! I talked to somebody ... it was ... I just don't remember. I was more than a little drunk."

"Where might it have been? At that hour?"

"That's right! Only Twenty Four was open! It had to be there! I was drunk, so they'll probably remember ... but I don't think I caused any trouble. Damn! Wish I'd started a row, huh?"

"Do you know Edna Barnes? Angie....."

"That's right! It was Angie! She made me drink the coffee! Said it wouldn't sober me any, but it would wake me up enough to get home! I talked to Angie at the Twenty Four!"

"Thanks. That gives two of you an alibi. Angie was with you, you were with her – at the time of the murder. Nothing else implied."

"I wish! I think I was too drunk to have done anything, anyway."

Tom came back on. GJ said to bring Raul in.

He was missing something obvious, and knew it. There was a nagging feeling centered around that car, somehow. He would go look at it, himself, as soon as the interviews were over.

Raul remained on the list. At home in bed alone was no alibi. He could have done it, but GJ didn't think so. He would have made it take longer and been more painful. Wrangle had seduced his girlfriend, resulting in an argument where the girlfriend broke up with him.

Pepe Gonzalez had a shaky. It depended on a brother and sister who would alibi him, no matter what. He had a violent temper, but he was another who GJ thought would just beat Wrangle to a pulp, not twist a wire around his throat. Still on, but very shaky.

Tara Glorine was a sullen, acid, scorned woman. She would be one who would cut it off for him and leave him to live with that. On the list, but just barely.

There was no getting around it, he would have to interview Cartwright more in depth. He did not relish that for one second. It was too hard a job not to smack him in the puss on general principles.

He was at the church. It would be a bit of psychological help to interview him there. He would be less inclined to lie about anything, while feeling he was on the high ground, in several ways.

"Tom, I'm going to talk with the Right Reverend. I don't think he did it, but he's damned hard to eliminate. I know what his answers will be, I just have to see if maybe one of them doesn't fit."

"Yeah. He was home. In bed, where anyone not Satan's own disciple was at two to three in the morning, Hallelujah and amen!"

He got the bird for that.

Maria called that Tom should go to Grantley and Forester. Two car collision. Fender bender. Everybody innocent.

"Forester is a stop street," Tom said.

"And?"

That got her the finger.

GJ went into the church, where Cartwright was meeting with four women on some kind of fund-raising committee. GJ said he'd wait, he just had a few things to clear up.

"I have nothing to hide. We may discuss anything not of a promised confidentiality here.. The Lord will be my witness as to truthfulness and verity." He sounded so pious GJ wanted to smack him. He would have to control the urge to expose him in front of those women.

"It's not that kind of thing. It's about general remembrances and connecting things."

"Such as?"

"Well, an instance in a park where certain matters were discussed and the person about whom the discussion centered was there to speak with me about it before I left the park. She explained the circumstances and doesn't care if she's connected with it. She had as much as solved that problem on her own, which could be expected, considering her personality."

"Hmpfth! I saw you talking to that Downy *person*!" a woman spat. "I suppose you wanted to know if she confessed to something tawdry she's done.

"Well! We don't have confession here! I would think a sheriff would know that much! We don't confess to a priest. Our confessions are directly to God!"

"You are?" GJ asked.

"I'm Mrs. Aida Johnson, treasurer at the Children's Education Fund of the Light of Hope Church of Mathonamesales, New Mexico, for your information."

"It would be Mrs. Evan Johnson or Mrs. Robert Johnson?"

"What?" she sounded confused.

"You are Aida Johnson or Mrs. Somebody Johnson."

"I didn't, why, I never, how rude!"

"Now, now, my dear," Cartwright said. "He is correct in conventional society that the married name is Mrs. name of husband. Mrs. means 'wife of.' It is correct to call yourself Aida Johnson, but not Mrs. Aida Johnson, unless your husband is deceased.

"I'm quite sure the sheriff meant no disparagement. Such things are often demanding of exactitude in all legal matters, and he is a representative of the legal part of government.

"The Lord has cautioned us to not take statements made in innocence as derogatory. My experiences with the sheriff and his deputy, even the good woman who runs the office, are that they are all honorable, if some are personally misguided, in a spiritual sense, which lacks much meaning, as they are simply doing, I might say, a very excellent job in difficult circumstances. We must be tolerant of things that are too often misunderstandings, not so much of the words, but of the intent of those words.

"The sheriff, as he is required to do by law, was merely establishing actual identity."

I can expect a sermon with each answer. Shit! I can't go after his obsequious ass here. I was outsmarted. By myself.

"That is true. I thank the reverend for explaining.

"Miss Downy was explaining that Reverend Cartwright was never involved in anything illegal, is all. *She* had no bad words to say about anyone. Quite the contrary. She had only very good things to say about the reverend. She was making it plain that something someone else reported about the reverend was untrue, that he greatly exceeded what was said, in the better sense of the words.

"Quite frankly, she was explaining that the reverend was in no way guilty of illegal acts. She was there, and she could attest to the truth of that. Not one thing illegal. Not a hint of any illegal thing."

"That is true. Miss Downy has, er, confessed, in her own way, that she is sometimes a bit outside of true Christian teachings, that accusations made about a situation can far too often be interpreted in negative ways. To allow that to continue does great harm to another. That is hardly a Christian act! We are admonished constantly by the Lord, Himself, to beware of false accusations, to always give the benefit of any doubt, in cases where there is doubt. It is what we are instructed to do by our Lord and Savior."

"Amen!" the women said, in unison.

"We have all done things that would be hard to explain, that would be a terrible embarrassment, if believed to have happened in an unacceptable way, now haven't we? Be honest! Have you never said or done something that would be an embarrassment, that you wished with your whole being had never been said or done? Have you? Have I?

"Yes! In all honesty, I have said and done things I felt and feel must be forgiven for me to ever know meaningful peace!

"Honesty, my friends! Can you look God in the eye and say you have never said or done things that were terrible, in your own conception?

"But God will understand the frailties of the flesh, of the human mind, of intentions! And God will forgive, if there is true remorse! Amen! Praise God!"

Shit! He's working them into a frensy!

The women were rocking from side to side and crying, "Amen! Hallelujah! Praise God!"

"Well, I don't have any more questions at this time. I apologize for interrupting your meeting. I have to go."

Cartwright was actually smirking. GJ bit back a vicious little stab he could have made then. He raised an eyebrow and smirked back, then left. Cartwright didn't look nearly so smug, all of a sudden.

He went to the garage. He called Tom, who brought him the keys.

"GJ, I've heard a thing or two about Phil Collins. There are some questions about whether parts were actually used that were paid for. That kind of thing. It might bear a little look-see, in itself."

"I heard a thing or two about that place, myself. Collins was in Taos that night. Confirmed."

Tom nodded. "I have to check on something. I think that fender bender was staged, but I can't think why. Maybe to keep us away from something else?"

"There wasn't something else to keep us away from ... but was there an insurance policy?"

"That was next choice. Gomez kept rubbing his neck, and once was staggering around a bit."

"Damage that could have caused anything?"

"No. A dent I could probably pound out with my fist."

"Write a report that says that. The damage was minimal and Gomez seemed to be acting. Make something about the angle of the blow or something that would indicate it was staged."

"I did put in that the angle was from in front and to the left side, so there was no possibility of whiplash from so small a contact."

"Have a copy on the front desk. Put a note to Maria that you expect an insurance adjustor ... what insurance company?"

"H, H, and H. Lmtd."

"So. They were suspected of setting up that kind

of thing and splitting the payoff. Have Maria write down the date of issuance of the policy. I'll bet Gomez didn't have any insurance until the last month, at most. He couldn't afford anything but the state policy."

Tom grinned. "Maybe the sheriff's department is suspicious, and this is plain blatant. Henderson, Henderson and Henderson might well sit in a cell for ninety days before their license is revoked, followed by investigation by the insurance companies they were ripping off. Got it!"

GJ turned to the garage. The keys were for the main door and a side door. He went to the side and in.

Well, there it was. What was it going to tell him?

It was truly a beautiful restoration. It looked like it had never been off the showroom floor.

GJ looked over the car very carefully from outside, took careful pictures at all angles, and moved to open the driver's door. He could see the evidence where Tom had taken prints.

He wasn't sure why he was doing this. Tom would have made a thorough job of it. There was just a nagging feeling at the back of his mind about that car. Consciously, he couldn't see a connection.

He stopped, then called Maria to have the former ownership of the car checked. It was possible the car *was* involved! Wrangle had been killed outside an auto repair shop!

He asked her if Tom's report found any prints, other than Wrangle's.

"No. Not even his."

Well, the car was clean and polished. That could be, but there would have been prints on the door handle. Why were those wiped?

He checked inside. Nothing.

He opened the trunk. Nothing.

He popped the hood. Nothing – or was there something? That carburetor was brand spanking new, but was the same make and model of the original. GJ had gone through the receipts, and there was nothing such in them. There was only the oil change, some antifreeze, and filters, plus the gas receipts. Wrangle had kept all receipts.

GJ thought a minute, then went to look at the work counter.

There were two deeply worn brake drums and one brake rotor, plus pads all around. There was a used caliper.

That was about four hundred bucks for all the original equipment matches. More.

No receipts?

Brake parts. The caliper was from the passenger side.

GJ jacked up the right front and took off the tire. There it was. He didn't need to check the rear.

So. All he had overlooked from the first was the solution. The killer had even gone so far as to bring up what was going on, a distraction that had worked. For awhile.

Jimmy Tate watched as the perfectly restored GTO drove off, and grinned. That was good for two hundred fifty! Phil was, as usual four days a week, in Taos. More for his girlfriend than the business. This would be gravy!

Edna Gladstone drove in in her Tacoma for the oil change. He did that, collected, gave her the receipt, and waved as she drove out, half an hour later.

Kenny Whitecloud came in in the old truck to say the left front brake was grabbing. Jimmy explained that it needed a new rotor, that he couldn't turn it again. It was already less than the law required. He made arrangements for time payments. Phil would have to bring a rotor from Taos. Day after tomorrow.

That Mustang went by. It was even more exact than the goat.

It came back and turned in. He would get a closeup look at a real classic! That was two in the area.

Wrangle, the asshole who owned it, did his own work. Why would he come ... parts. That was going to turn into another gold mine for Jimmy Tate!

Needed two drums and kits and a new rotor and caliper. They had all that in stock. It had been back there for a couple of years or more. Jimmy got the parts and added up the bill on his calculator. Four hundred seventy two plus tax.

"I can give you a discount and no tax if you don't need a receipt?"

"How much?" from Wrangle.

"Even four."

Wrangle thought a minute, then made a phone call, didn't get an answer, then took four hundreds from his wallet and had Jimmy tell him exactly why he was offered a deal like that.

"Parts aren't exactly in the 'most often sold' file. We had them. I cut the margin in half and we don't have them taking up space here anymore. It would be ten years before you need a new set, and then might get them in Taos or somewhere. They'd cost double by then, if you could even find them. Everybody gets a deal, and the state gets too much anymore, anyhow."

Wrangle nodded, put the parts in the trunk, and drove out.

Banner day! If he could keep this going for awhile he'd buy and restore his own classic!

The goat had just driven out. Eighty five bucks. Phil was in Taos. Wrangle had been talking with Higgins while Jimmy got the parts. They were talking about some girl, not the cars. Jimmy handed Higgins his tranny cable and link connectors and collected. Jimmy winked at Wrangle, who was talking on his phone.

Wrangle needed a new carb. It wasn't anything they had around, so Phil would have to bring it from Taos. It and the tranny cable would go on the insurance list. Things that had to be brought in – that Phil didn't know about before – went on the theft list. The adjustor never asked questions. There wasn't that much for a business this size in this kind of place.

Jimmy called Phil, who was at the distributor. It would be next week or ten days. The carb had to be special ordered.

Wrangle okayed it.

Wrangle left. Sheila Carstairs and Amy Browneagle came in to giggle and flirt. They were both knockouts. He was damned glad he had enough "extra income" to be able to afford them.

The insurance adjuster came in. He checked over the few things and noted the thefts were, in almost half the cases, for older classic models, and that there were only a couple in the area.

"Yeah. We keep the stuff for them, but only a few parts. First thing I did was check on if they had any new parts around, but they only had what they bought here and in Taos, and had receipts. I think maybe somebody is waiting for them to need some kind of rare part they can sell them for a bundle. I have ears out for if anybody says anything about that kind of stuff."

"I think they know what parts they want and take them into Houston. There're a lot of classic collectors there. One or two never buy parts. They have shops and claim they make their own, but it isn't all original if they make it, is it, so it gets your doubts in high gear!"

They chatted awhile, then the guy left. Jimmy gave his back the bird and smirked. Built-in answer – for an idiot!

Kyle Friendly came in. He wanted to know how much it would cost for new tires for Tim Blackclaw's truck. He was nervous about them being so worn, and Tim was such a good friend he would like to do something for him.

You'd like to do something to him! Probably do. That's why you consider him such a good friend.

He quoted a price from the catalogue. Four for two fifteen. Individual price $76.29. That was better than he had hoped! The truck would be there in about an hour!

Phil came back four hours later with parts. He was a little drunk, which was another great thing to Jimmy. He forgot about things when he'd had a few.

"I wish you wouldn't drink when you drive," Jimmy said. "I worry about you."

"I'll need a gas tank gage," Wrangle said. "I can pick it up on my way home from the club Wednesday night. It's late, but you'll be up with those two beauties. I do okay, but I'm a little jealous! They won't go for it with me!"

"They're expensive, but I can tell you straight-out they're worth it!"

They talked a bit. It was true it wouldn't be any problem to deliver the stuff at two thirty in the morning if the payment was there. After all, he couldn't afford the women without those payments!

Wrangle left, and Jimmy checked the Hollander for the gage. It fit a lot of things, and there were four that would interchange. Nobody on an authentication board would check inside the gas tank.

The one for that make and model was $52.50. The interchange they had in back cost $14.29. He would tape over the MM on the box and put ... no. He'd put it in a plastic bag with a tag that it was the real MM and put it inside the sealed bag. He knew how to seal plastic. Give him a discount.

$40.07. Make it a weird number and they believe it.

Andres Velasquez came in for oil and filters. Hank Fordyce came in for ditto. George Hawkcaller came in for a tune-up. It was a pretty good day, all-in-all.

Lenny was back to help. He'd taken a vacation while it was slow time of the year. He chatted about meeting Phil in Taos and about going to Mexico and getting drunk on tequila. He'd only taken twenty bucks that they would be able to find. He'd slept with a hot Mexican chick, who stole the twenty, of course. That was cheaper than the whores, who charged from fifty to a hundred. Lenny could open in the morning and check the place over. He could sleep an extra half hour.

Jimmy wasn't altogether sober, but he also wasn't drunk, by a good margin.

Wrangle called and said he'd be at the shop in ten minutes. Jimmy went in the back door to get the gage. He picked up a length of baling wire and a hammer to use to hang a couple of pictures in his place. It could use some kind of decorations and there were spots on the walls that could be covered.

Wrangle came to get the gage. He said he wouldn't be paying for anymore parts. Jimmy would end up in jail if he didn't supply anything he asked. He had taken videos of the former transactions on his Ipad.

Jimmy didn't think. He had the hammer in his hand and smacked Wrangle in the head with the side of it. Wrangle dropped. Jimmy was so furious he wrapped the wire around his neck and twisted it tight.

He was scared, then. He went back inside, put the hammer back in the drawer, put the gage in the original box, and put it back on the shelf. He shoved the tag and plastic bag into a used oil filter and dropped it in the drum, checked to see no one was about, went out and locked the door, saw the Blackberry laying there, picked it up, and slid it into his pocket, and went home.

He would be caught. He just knew it!

Well, GJ said, a lot of times, that he would go damned easy on anyone who killed a blackmailer. He could hope he meant it.

He was surprised when he woke up that he had even been able to sleep. A few minutes later Lenny called and said there was a dead guy out back of the shop. Jimmy said to call the police. He's be right there.

"Tom, we overlooked the obvious, I think. We knew a few things we never connected," GJ explained. "We knew that Wrangle was into restoring a classic car, and we knew Phil's sold parts and got special order packages when he was in Taos. We knew there was theft from the shop. We knew Wrangle was a blackmailer.

"It came together when I saw those parts in the garage and there were no receipts for them.

"Where was Wrangle's phone? It wasn't on the body, and it wasn't in his house or car or garage. He was seen using it by everyone, but it was gone? Why? No one around here would kill anyone for a phone, and it wasn't even a particularly expensive one.

"How else can you add that up?"

"I see. Phil, who was in Taos, Lenny, who wasn't in a position to get away with much, or Jimmy, who was.

"What do you suppose set it off?"

"I don't know, but it's a good bet it had something to do with blackmail. Maybe Wrangle got parts and recorded it on that phone, then was going to blackmail Jimmy about it. We would have to find how Jimmy got him there to kill him."

"Told him he had some kind of part or something that had to be gone before morning," Maria said.

"I think a blackmailer wouldn't fall for anything like that," Tom said. "You are blackmailing someone who calls and says to meet them in a place where no one would see you at two o'clock in the morning? Not going to happen."

"I think it was something that Wrangle set up," GJ said. "A blackmailer could set something like that up. It might have been something that backfired on him We'll have to ask."

"We have to be able to tie it tighter than that," Maria warned. "You have fifty doubts a lawyer could bring up."

"That's the roadblock. There wasn't a print on

the car, and ... that wouldn't mean anything. Wrangle could have, probably did, wipe everything off, himself, when he polished it."

"We don't have what he was hit with. If it was Jimmy, it will be in the shop," Tom pointed out.

GJ nodded, but wasn't hopeful. There had to be hundreds of things in that shop that would stun a person if hit in the head with them – not to mention there was enough time to get rid of whatever it was.

"Well ... we never found that phone. You just said that," Maria put in.

"We did find the number!" Tom cried. "We can call and see who answers!"

GJ smirked. "Not yet. Chances are that phone's not in this county anymore, but a small chance it is.

"Let's go to the shop. If Jimmy's there, we can call. If the phone's in the shop and not turned off, it will ring. We have him."

Tom and GJ went to the shop. Jimmy was there, as were Lenny and Phil. GJ talked with them. Tom made a phone call that rang, but wasn't answered. Jimmy looked very nervous.

"Okay, Jimmy. Can we go to your place and talk, or do I have to serve the warrant?" GJ asked.

"Warrant? We can talk right here. What's it about?"

"I'll go to your apartment while you talk here, but I'd think you would rather talk more in private," Tom said.

Jimmy shook his head and looked much more scared.

"What happened? He was putting the screws to you and you struck out? Why did you kill him?"

Jimmy just shook his head.

"Okay. I'll go to your apartment to look around. Here's the warrant," Tom said.

Jimmy didn't say anything. He stood and waved at the door. They went out while Phil and Lenny looked totally confused.

They went into the apartment. Jimmy said he didn't know what they thought they would find there. There wasn't anything.

Tom made a phone call. There wasn't any sound ... except a slight buzzing from the kitchen. They went into the kitchen and Tom started to call again. Jimmy went to the cutlery drawer and took out a fancy Blackberry to hand to GJ. He didn't say anything. The phone was on vibrate.

"You should have turned it off," Tom said. "It ties it. We have you."

"I should have smashed it up into dust with a sledge hammer!" Jimmy replied. "It has videos on it."

"Blackmail evidence?" GJ asked.

"Yeah. Me and some others."

"You'll confess?"

"I guess I already did. Yeah."

"Oops!" GJ cried, and dropped the Blackberry. He sort of jumped and his boot heel hit the phone squarely. Parts flew around for a couple of feet. He picked up the master board and took out the memory chip, which he "accidentally" dropped. His heel came down on it. He twisted the heel when he spun around to ask, "Did either of you see where it went?"

"Where what went?" Tom asked.

"Will I get bail? I have a couple thousand dollars in the dresser, under my shorts," Jimmy asked.

"Wish I could say yes, but probably not," GJ answered.

"You're a really decent person, aren't you?" Jimmy asked. "What happens to me?"

"It was about a crime, so I guess you'll be charged with manslaughter," GJ replied. "He presented you with blackmail evidence and you struck out."

"That's what happened."

"I think you'll get minimum. You have to make it up to Phil about the parts."

"The insurance did that. I guess I'll have to pay them back for all of it, but only part was me."

"H, H, and H?" Tom asked.

"Henderson. Yeah."

"I don't think they'll want to make any noise. They're into schemes, themselves."

"The whole damned world is!" Jimmy said.

They got a few things together and went to the station. Jimmy was booked. Reports were filed. At six o'clock the night shift came on and the day crew went home.

GJ got up and turned off the alarm before it went off.

He did the morning routine, then headed for the station. Maria was already there. Tom was on vacation, starting today. The trial was an uncontested confession where all Tom, Maria and GJ had to do was confirm the evidence. GJ and Tom both stressed that Jimmy had struck out in panic at a blackmailer.

The lawyer tried to give the judge a silly story about Jimmy only remembering going to the shop after midnight and waking up in bed the next morning, when part of it came back.

Jimmy said that part wasn't really true, that he remembered hitting Wrangle with the hammer and remembered standing up and sort of twisting the wire that he had in his hand for hanging pictures.

That went a long way toward making the decision. A defendant calling his lawyer on a stretching of the truth to on the line of a lie. That, and when the judge asked if Wrangle had attacked him in any way.

"No, other than with a threat. He didn't try to hit me or anything."

"Guilty, with mitigating circumstances. One year of community service and time served. Next case."

Phil said he could take the time for community service off, but he would have to promise no more theft.

Maria couldn't believe it!

"What the hell?" Phil said. "He's the only mechanic around here I can say knows his ass from a cowflop! He didn't do anything every other employee I've ever had did!

"Well, except for getting rid of a low class piece of shit."

Phil had treated them all to a good lunch.

Not the lawyer. Had Jimmy not "corrected" him, he would have gotten two years.

Maria came into the office about half an hour later. He was just putting the final reports in the file cabinet.

"You have a visitor."

GJ raised an eyebrow.

"My dear friends, I wish to speak with the sheriff about something that has eventuated in our little town to cause deep concern..."

"Oh, groan! Not Cartwright!"

"Part of the job." He gave her the finger.

Cartwright came in.

"And a gracious good morning to you, my dear friend! The Lord has smiled upon our little community and has delivered justice for those iniquities practiced by a truly depraved and evil soul! We must thank the Good Lord for bringing this ..."

"Yeah. Okay. What do you want?"

"Er, it would seem that there has been a bit of, how shall I state it? A bit of unwanted intrusion into the properties of the..."

"A break-in?"

"Indeed! An intrusion into the very sanctum of the..."

"At the church?"

"As I have declared, an evil and uninvited intrusion..."

"What was stolen?"

"Theft, in the legal sense, was not the intention of this disciple, or those disciples, of Satan! The destruction of the blessed..."

"They broke some things up."

"And the depictions and scripts of the incarnate..."

"And they wrote some things. On the walls?"

"Oh, the deceitful, dishonest, depraved rantings of the..."

"Yeah. Okay. Maria will take a statement and

we'll investigate."

"The Good Lord will bless and protect the servants of honor and truth, those who uncover the evils perpetrated upon the Godly. He will protect and defend..."

"But he was busy when they broke in and wrote on the walls. We'll get to it.

"Forgive me for the shortness. I am involved in an investigation, at the moment. We will investigate your case as quickly and completely as possible." *I'm busy investigating what insanity made me take this job!*

Cartwright finally left. Maria came in to ask if they had a case.

"Well, a case of what? Religious fervor?

"I guess we do. It's out job to investigate complaints of vandalism for even that kind of thing."

"Shit!"

"That about sums it up."

C. D. Moulton's works are available on most major outlets as printed or e-books. CD writes the CD Grimes, PI, mysteries, the Det. Lt. Nick Storie mysteries, the Clint Faraday mysteries, the Flight of the Maita science fiction series, books on orchid culture and many others of many types. Mystery, adventure, intrigue, science fiction, humor, fantasy, paranormal, mild erotica, and factual.